Preachers That Prey

M. Nigel Wright

DEDICATION

I dedicate this book to all of you. To the people whom have supported me from day one. I have much love for you all.
Thanks are only a fraction of how I feel.
Continue to blow me up on social media.

Sincerely, Moses.

CONTENTS

ACKNOWLEDGMENTS

alex-robinson-AGr13YPOPqw-unsplash.

enrique-guzman-egas-6MxaJTKQzOo-unsplash

ron-smith-tknOyEefp2k-unsplash

Cover art created by: Moses Wright

CHAPTER ONE

Praise the Lord Saints!

"Praise the Lord," yelled the congregation.

"It is truly an honor and a privilege to be in the house of the Lord today", Pastor McQueen replied.

I stand here before you today with a tremendous smile on my face. For two reasons I am smiling right now. I have been blessed to serve you and God for the last forty-one years. I am proud of all the things that we have accomplished during this time. We started here with a tiny, little old store front church and have grown to over six hundred members and if you'll keep having all these babies: it'll be seven hundred by Christmas time.

As some of you know, I've been speaking about retirement now for quite some time. Thanks be to God, that time has finally arrived. Now don't you'll fret none because the second reason I am smiling is that God has already sent us a replacement and you all have voted unanimously to put him right to work for the church.

He has served here under my direction for a couple of years, and God has shown his power through this young man. I still don't know how he does some of the things that he does. All I know is that God is truly in the mist of it all.

"Come on up here Brother Marcus," Yelled the Pastor.

Let everyone greet you with a warm welcome hug and smile. Ladies and Gentlemen, I present to you your new Ex Minister and now Rev. Marcus Moore.

"Ushers will you bring the folks around that want to come and shake his hand?" asked Pastor McQueen.

Now you'll single women in here, don't try to hug him too hard. I'm watching you with Holy eyes. We are all trying to find the new reverend a wife but that's still God's work. He'll get hitched in time.

"Don't none of you get mad if God don't pick you," said Pastor.

They all came around and greeted him. The church was so excited and relieved. They were afraid that they might not find a new pastor. Pastor McQueen was very up in age and he had taken the church as far as he could.

They needed something or someone with fresh new ideas and vision for the church's ministry and they felt that Rev. Marcus Moore exhibited all the talent and know how to take them further.

Once the service was over Pastor and Rev. Moore had a short meeting in his office. Pastor was a direct man.

"Now look here Marcus are you sure you are ready for this hell?" pastor asked.

Marcus couldn't do anything but laugh for the moment.

"Pastor I'm sure that whatever I'm facing in the future will require lots and lots of prayer," Marcus responded.

Still with that in mind, I feel that God has prepared me for this mission.

"OK now young negro", pastor replied.

Those fools out there will cut you down, eat you up and throw you out to the dogs for some of the smallest bullshit. You will one Sunday just pronounce a word in the Bible wrong and you'll have some ignorant bastard wanting to demote you.

"I'm just telling you son that it ain't going to be easy no matter how much God you have in you," said Pastor.

"Another thing, do you own a gun?" asked Pastor.

"No sir," Marcus responded.

"Well you might want to consider getting one", Pastor told him.

I keep mine on me all the time. Young man, times have changed and it ain't getting any better. I'm not going to God calls me, not when some jealous blind fool calls my name.

So, protect yourself and do me a big favor if you would.

"What's that Pastor?" asked Marcus.

"Start a singles committee and find out where all these children are coming from with no fathers", replied Pastor.

It doesn't look good when people come and visit the church. They see all these pretty women and few little men.

"I'll get right on that Pastor McQueen," say Marcus.

"Alright, now get out of my office," say Pastor.

I need to change out of this robe and put on my eating clothes. Sister Amy and them going to the BBQ house and they are paying. All I have to do is bless the food, and I'm good at that.

CHAPTER TWO

I took in all that Pastor had told me that Sunday evening. I knew that I was in store for a rough ride. I also knew that I worked too hard to get here, and I needed "my" vision to evolve.

I guess you say, "What is my vision and what does that have to do with anything?"

Well, let me go back close to the beginning where it all started.

I am Marcus Moore. I grew up in a home with three sisters, my dad, and my mother. You can say that we were ok. I mean we weren't poor, but we were nowhere near middle class. My father worked two jobs to take care of us. He worked in an auto manufacturing plant during the week and on weekends he would work at the schools buffing floors and painting. He was a kind man which makes me sometimes upset with my mother. I would watch my father come home beat to the ground and my mother would start in on him. He loved her dearly, but I know some days he wanted to knock her ass out cold.

My dad gave my mother all she needed and more and I would sometimes hear them through the walls of our home arguing. I guess my dad would be a little horny and wanted some attention from my mom. She would claim that she was tired and tell him to go to sleep. He cursed and ramped until she'd finally give in.

Then one night my mom said those dreadful words to my dad. Here is how it went down.

"Come on Barbara now why I got to keep asking you for ass that is supposed to be mine?" dad asked.

"Melvin I'm so tired of you", Mom replied. I'm not your sex doll to screw every night.

"Well damn Barbara, you suppose to be my wife", he said.

Do I need to go and get a damn sex doll or may another damn woman?

I'm getting kind of fed up now Barbara.

"Ok Melvin", mom said. You make me so sick. Come on and "HURRY UP!"

Why did my mom say those words? I don't know, but it sent my dad into a frenzy fit. I heard him tell my mother that it would be cold day in hell before he asked her for any more ass.

My sisters and I listened as my dad seemed to be getting dress.

We heard my mother ask, "where you going this time of night?"

"The hell out of here", dad replied.

I do so much for you and those kids Barbara. I work two jobs and take care of this house. You don't have to lift a finger around here. You drive around in your little nice car like you are the shit. Then you spend the rest of your time neglecting your husband.

"Well no more Barbara", dad yelled.

We could hear him walking through the house. It was very loud this time like thunder, so we knew that he was pretty mad at mother.

"Bye kids", dad yelled.

"I'm sure you could hear everything," he said.

Marcus let this be a lesson to you son. You can never please a damn woman especially a black one. You give them the world, but they can't give you no pussy!

We heard him kick something and then we heard the door slam. It was about eleven at night. No one knew where dad was going. A few minutes passed, and we came out of our rooms.

Mom was sitting in the living room on the couch. She wasn't crying or anything. She did look pretty mad, though. She looked up at us as just stared for about a minute.

She dropped her head and said, "Go to bed."

We did get back into bed, but I don't think that anyone got any sleep. Our minds were racing with thoughts. Is dad ever coming back? Are they going to get a divorce? Are we going to have to move? It was a very tense night for sure.

The next morning when we got up, we saw that mother had fallen asleep on the couch. I guess that she was hoping to be there if dad came home. Dad did not come home last night nor did he call.

My sisters were older than I was and they took me into the kitchen to fix breakfast. No one spoke a single word. Mother must have heard us and she went back into the bedroom and closed the door. We just sat there and ate cereal in silence.

I couldn't hold it anymore. I asked my sisters "Are all of you like that?"

My oldest sister Chenille asked, "What do you mean all of you Marcus?" She was not smiling when she asked.

Daddy said that you can't please a black woman. All of you are black women.

All three of my sisters looked at me with angry faces. The response I received was not what I was waiting for.

"You are going to be one of those Negros that only date white girls Marcus?" Chenille asked.

I bet you are. You look like that kind of person. You got your mother's skin color and your Dad's hair. You all pretty Negros usually don't go for the sisters.

Oh, did I mention that I was mixed race?

My dad is Puerto Rican with Black and my mother is all Black. So I had the brown skin to be all black, but I had hair like my dad. It was deep black with major waves.

I use to wonder why the girls would play in my hair in grade school. I always thought that it was stupid to like someone for their looks, but that's how foolish girls can be. I didn't know why my sisters were mad, though. They had the same features as I but just different.

They had mom's thighs and hips and they had dad's hair too. They look like black girls who may have had Indians in their family. So how could they cut me down?

Anyway, I told my sisters "no. I love black women."

I thought that would ease the tension, but I could see and feel the vibes coming my way. It was like they wanted to hate on me.

I quickly ate my cereal and went to my room. I started cleaning my room which was a Saturday morning ritual in our house. Mom and dad did not play that nasty house game. We all cleaned on Saturday morning.

We heard the chime to the garage door. We knew that it was dad. I got as close to my door as I could hear what might go down.

I could tell that my sisters had stopped cleaning too. We heard him come in and open the refrigerator. That meant that he was grabbing a beer.

It was weird because dad usually works at the school on Saturdays. He loved his little side hustle job. I know he loved seeing Miss Regina who also worked there on the weekend. She adored my dad. I guess it was just a crush because Miss Regina was a married woman.

We heard him walk down the hallway, and he opened that door that led to the attic. My dad had converted that upper area into his man cave. It was very nice up there but we weren't allowed unless he said we could come in. It had a big screen TV and a nice futon couch bed. Dad had it made up there away from the world.

He didn't check on mom, and mom did not come out of her room to greet him. After we heard the TV come on we just continued with our cleaning.

The hold day had passed and soon my dad came from up stairs. He looked at me with a smile as he entered the living room. As he passed me, I could tell that he had been drinking heavily. I could smell it strong like it was coming out of his pores. I didn't bother to say a word. You never can guess the mood of someone like that.

He went into the kitchen and made a plate of leftovers. When he started the microwave, my mother walked in. Dad never looked her way. "There's some corn bread in the oven if you want some," she said.

My dad never uttered a word. He acted as if she was never there. Mom repeated her statement but dad never responded to her.

He grabbed his plate from the microwave and another beer and headed back upstairs. I could see the look on my mother's face. You know the look a child has when they know they really messed up this time?

Well, that's the look my mother wore on her face. She got her water bottle and went back to their bedroom.

Sunday church was another weekend ritual in our home. We attended church service faithfully like clockwork. It was different this time, though. We gathered in the living room waiting for our father to come down. The door to upstairs never opened. Mom and dad have had spats before, but they never missed church over it.

Somehow church seemed to help heal the tension between them but this time would be different.

"Come on kids", mother said. We can't keep the Lord waiting.

The ride to church was awkward in every way. I thought again about mom and dad divorcing and then I'd think about what my sisters said the day before. All I knew is I was scared of white girls.

As the service went on, I could tell that my mother's thoughts were a million miles away from church. We have seen my father upset but not to this degree. I wondered if my mother was thinking the same thing as we were. She'd try to smile and participate in the preaching, but I knew better.

When alter call started, my mother got up and went to the front. My sisters and I just looked at it each other all wide eyed. You never go up front unless you were in big trouble and only God could get you out of it.

Mom would always say "I'm not going up there so people can be all in my business." We knew it was serious this time for mom to do this.

Going back home was like waiting for a court sentence to be handed down. You could hear a pin drop in that car. No one looked at each other. We just looked straight ahead. Mom stopped at the store and asked us to wait in the car. When she returned, we could see that she also bought dad another pack of beer. I guess she was trying to lighten the mood when she gets home.

When we walked into the house, dad was coming out of the master bedroom. He never said a word as he proceeded back upstairs. Mom placed the beer in the kitchen and went straight to her room. My siblings and I did what normally took place on Sunday. We'd get out of our church clothes, do schoolwork and wait for dinner to be prepared.

A couple of hours went by, and it was all quiet in our home.

Mom yelled, "Dinner's ready everyone."

I'm sure she meant that "everyone" comment for my dad to hear.

We washed up and entered the kitchen in single file.

We sat down and my mom said, "Marcus, please bless the food."

I asked if we should wait for dad and she just gave me a blank stare. I read between the lines on that one quickly. I began to pray over the food, and I ended the prayer with asking God not to let my mother and father split up. My dad entered the kitchen just as I said that.

He stopped and bowed his head for me to continue the prayer. Amazingly he said Amen when the rest of us said it. He never looked at my mother though, but I could see her peek up at him a couple of times. She missed his playfulness.

My dad fixed his plate, grabbed another beer, and headed right back upstairs. That was the sign to me that it was over. We always had Sunday dinner together as a family. Come rain or shine, my parents spent every Sunday evening together since before I was born. I lost my appetite after that moment.

"Marcus, you may be excused", mom said.

I understand, and I see it all over your face. The rest of you can stay and eat or whatever you wish. Then she got up holding back tears. My mother ran to her room. We could hear her burst into a crying bliss.

What can I say other than Life went goes on?

One day we came home from my auntie's house, and dad had loaded up his truck. Our uncle William was there I guess to help him move his things. He never looked at my mother. I felt that if he ever looked at her, he would somehow break down and change his mind about things.

My mother walked over and spoke to my uncle.

I heard my uncle whisper "I'm sorry Barbara."

My mother never said a word. She walked up behind my dad and just stood there for a minute.

"If this is what you must do Melvin, then so be it", mom said. Just know that I love you, and I always will.

"You're a good man Melvin," she said.

I just wish I treated you better before you got to this point.

My dad never responded but I saw the water in his eyes. He never looked up, but I looked up at him and he was fighting it hard. Nevertheless, He never stopped packing.

We went in and dad came in the house to hug all of us. He never hugged mom, though. He told us to be strong and always do the right thing no matter what happens to us. That sounded kind of strange because I wanted to know if he was doing the right thing right now.

My mother just stood there and looked at him.

Dad grabbed the last two beers from the refrigerator and headed out the front door. He did not look back.

Dad would stop by on weekends to see us and bring us gifts but never for mom. They had not spoken in about two months now. My sisters and I have accepted the fact that our parents were not getting back together.

I hated it I because I was in the house with four black women who now hated all black men. My sisters didn't say it to me, but I could hear them talking to my mother. I kept my distance away from them.

CHAPTER THREE

After about three years of being separated from my dad, my mother decides that we should move outside of Atlanta. She was tired of people asking what happened between her and dad. It was going on the holiday season, and she needed a change. She asked me to speak to my father and share the news. Dad was not really happy about it and told me to tell mother he will live with whatever decision she chooses to make. He said that he would move back into our home after we had moved out. It was only right because he was still paying the mortgage.

It seems that my mother had already been scouting a place to live. We were packed and out of the house in a few days.

It turned out to be a nice place. It wasn't as big as our previous home but I liked the look of the neighborhood.

We settled in quickly, and mom told us to be ready to register for school on Monday morning. Man, did my mind begin to race?

We arrived at the school around nine the morning. It was a big school and looked fairly new. My sisters were taken to their new class and soon it would be my turn.

The counselor shook my hand and asked me to come with her. It seemed like we walked for hours to get to the other side of the building. We stopped at the door to my class and the counselor whispered for the teacher to come into the hallway.

He came out, and he looked kind of fruity. He wore a loud purple shirt with a pink and purple bow tie. He was one of those guys that had that female voice type.

I shook Mr. Robert's hand, and he led me into the classroom. "Oh heavenly Father", I said.

There she was sitting there with her legs crossed.

She was the most beautiful lady I had ever seen in my young life. She was all I could focus on. I heard nothing that my new teacher was telling me.

"Young Marcus," He said. Let's stay focused for a moment.

Class I'd like to introduce you to our new student and classmate Mr. Marcus Moore. He comes to us by way of Atlanta, Georgia. Please let's welcome him with a warm applause.

The class clapped as I found my way to the nearest empty desk. I was in Heaven at least that is how I felt the rest of the day.

I had to play it cool, though. I was the new guy, and I didn't know if she was taken. Besides, if something jumped off, I didn't have any boys to back me up yet.

Lunch time came quick. I just followed everyone else acting like I knew the routine. At the same time, I was looking for her. I didn't know her name yet, so I say her.

I saw a set of small tables to the left, and I chose to sit there and eat my lunch. I guess they were tables for nerds or losers. It was cool because I was the new guy.

A couple of girls walked by and made comments like "Oh girl he got some pretty hair." I was used to that, so I ignored them. I was looking for my queen.

Just about that time, she entered the lunch room with two other girls. She looked right at me and kind of motioned the two girls to look why way. She fixed her tray and started coming towards me. She sat down two tables away so that she could look right at me.

I felt funny because the other girls kept turning around smiling. I had no clue of what was being said. All I know is that she was checking a brother out.

My next four classes were not with her, but she stayed

on my mind all day. My mother picked us up right on time. I didn't want her to see me getting in the car with three sisters. She may think that I'm one of those girly guys that act like my sisters.

"How was your first day kids?" mom asked
.

My sisters went on and on about the nice school and the classes they were in. That was good because I had to control my excitement. Mom didn't forget about me, though. She is thorough like that.

"What about you Marcus?" she asked.

"It was pretty cool mom," I replied.

"Did you make any new friends yet?" she asked.

"No ma'am, I'm chilling right now," I said.

"Mother he is lying though his teeth," my sister said.

There's a girl in my fourth period class that asked if I was his sister. She said there was a new cute guy in her first class that just stared at her all class long. She was saying that she might want to talk with him.

I could not speak. All I could do was smile. My sister was cool with the women I wanted to hook up with. Now my only dilemma was how I can get my sister to hook a brother up and stay out of my business at the same time. I didn't want this to start with my sister in the mix.

I later found out her name is Gloria from listening to my talkative siblings. I also learned that she was a cheerleader. I should have guessed at that one. All the pretty girls try out for cheerleading.

Now it was time to show my skills and try out for the basketball team. My mother was thrilled with that decision. She was a true sports fan.

They had a large assembly in the gym for the students to announce who made the quads. Of course Gloria's named was called, she was the captain. My sisters lost their mind when they heard my same came for position of point guard. Even Gloria cheered me on as I stood and accepted my jersey. I knew that Gloria and I would see a lot of each other the season.

I would play normal when we had home games. I didn't want to be the pretty boy show off. Tory was pretty upset that I got the point guard position. I felt that I worked really hard to get it.

I learned through the grape vine that not only did he want that position but he wanted Gloria too. He had been after her since elementary school. Gloria never gave him the time of day.

Now the away games were the times I would try to shine. Gloria would sit with me on the bus to and from the games. People would say that we made a great couple. We were coming from one away game, and the bus was rocking.

We won the district title, and man, were they celebrating. When I felt no one was watching or even cared, I made my move to kiss Gloria. It felt like she was expecting it. She grabbed the side of my face and wet me up with those gorgeous lips. I opened my eyes and all I could see was Tory staring angrily at me. He looked like he could explode.

"Don't worry about him, Marcus", Gloria said. He'll get over it one day.

I didn't see it that way. I knew how a man felt when the woman he loves shows him no attention. I made it my business to speak with him soon.

When we unloaded the gear from the bus, I told Tory that we needed to rap a minute. He agreed and told me that we'll talk after the showers. It felt like a tense moment. I didn't know how he was going to react later.

He came over to the lockers and sat on the bench waiting for me to finish getting dressed.

"What's up Marcus man?" Tory asked. What's so important that we need to talk?

"Tory don't play tough dog," I replied.

This is not that kind of conversation. I just wanted to break the ice between us man. I found out that you have had a crush on Gloria for years. How was I supposed to know that from my first day here? Plus, you and I haven't really spoken to each other since I joined the team. Don't you think that's kind of odd and looks a little stupid to everyone else?

"I'm cool with it man," he says.

Every since you kissed her, I've let it go. I don't want her now. I consider her spoiled meat. I don't want your sloppy second's dude.

"Wow, are you really going to go out like that Tory?" I asked.

How is it sloppy seconds and we have never had sex man? Bro you sound straight stupid right now.

Before I knew it, Tory swung at me. I leaned back and was able to grab his arm. I twisted his arm behind him and slammed him into the lockers. I told him not to ever try that again or that arm will end up broken. Some of the other guys came over to break us up.

"Guys, man this is not worth getting kicked off the team," one said.

I didn't think about that. I can't afford to be kicked off the team. What would that do for Gloria and me?

I enjoyed the bus trips and now the kisses. I let Tory go after that warning. He said nothing and walked away with his bag. I knew somehow that it wasn't over.

We took our winning all the way to the finals. The greatest part of that was it took us to North Carolina. I could really spend some time with Gloria without interference. We would be in North Carolina from Thursday until Monday. We only had to play two games in the tournament.

We stayed in a very nice hotel. Coach put the girls on one floor and the guys on another. That didn't matter because he never checked on anyone.

I don't know how, but someone got their hands on a bottle of alcohol. A couple of people decided to make a drunken punch. I never drank alcohol, so I knew I would not participate in whatever was going to happen. We gathered in one of the rooms and hung out. It was about seven of us in there. We did our best not to draw attention to the room.

They first started playing card games and then someone suggested a little spin the bottle. I declined on that but encouraged the others to go on. They were getting wild in there. All of them did not spin well and all ended up half-naked. There was a knock at the door, and it was Gloria. I let her in and she fell out laughing. She also declined on playing with them. She sat very close to me, almost in my lap.

I got really excited, and she could see my excitement in my shorts.

"Let's go get some ice Gloria," I said.

I needed a reason to leave out before everyone noticed my issue.

We got up, and she walked in front of me to hide my hard on. At the same time she held on to it squeezing it softly back and forth. We walked passed her room and she stopped me. She pushed me against the door and kissed the heck out of me. She then opened her hotel door and pulled me in her room.

Her roommate was with her boyfriend.

She looked and me and said "let me take care of that before you blow up."

She laid me down on her bed and pulled my short down a few inches. She gently pulled my penis out and began to stroke it. She then went into her bag and got her lotion. She put some in her hand and rubbed it across the head of my dick. She stroked soft and slow back and forth until I exploded in there. I had come before but never by the hands of someone else.

I felt so close to her after that episode. You could say that I was in love dude.

Gloria went into the bathroom and ran a rag in some hot water. She cleaned me up well and pulled my shorts back up.

"Are you better now sweetie?" she asked.

You were full dear. You won't have any problems making a baby one day and you sure won't have an issue pleasing a woman.

"That's for damn sure baby", she said.

We grabbed the ice and headed back to the room. Those clowns in there were so drunk from that punch. We beg them to keep the noise down, or we'd get in trouble. After a while we all returned to our rooms. We had the final game the next day, and we needed rest.

We played well but the other team played a little better. It felt great just to experience going to the playoffs. Coach didn't really seem upset that we lost. He told us that he was proud of us, and he looked forward to next season. Gloria and I enjoyed that weekend. I felt like I owed her for what she did for me in her room. I did want her to do it again soon.

Our relationship grew stronger and stronger. We were inseparable from one another. People could see that we were so in love. We started planning our life after high school. We picked our college we'd attend and everything.

I was so in love that my grades started falling. I was border line getting kicked off the team. All I could do was think about Gloria. How was I wiped, and I haven't had any pussy yet? I knew that I had to get my grades back up, though. My mother was getting pretty pissed off at me and my sisters cracked a million jokes when mom wasn't around.

"Did little miss pretty Gloria suck your dick"? Chenille asked.

I didn't know how to respond. She took my silence as a yes answer. They were never going to let me live that down now.

"You know that you have to return the favor now," she said. You have to go down on her now. You got to lick the split boyfriend.

Why were my sisters talking like this and where did they learn all of this crap? I walked into the kitchen for some water. My throat got real dry real fast.

"You want me took hook it up for you little brother?" she asked.

I can't have my favorite brother walking around school looking like a straight up punk. I'll invite her over to distract her parents and then I'll get mom out of the house for you. I know how to do it now.

I sat there surrounded by their smiling faces. My youngest sister was only eighteen. How did she know about this? She then admitted that she had a guy at school to lick her down there. She told me that it happened underneath the stairs near the home economics class. I was blown away by their remarks. They seem like scandalous old women. They talked about how they use their looks and ass shape to use men. They called men stupid and only want one thing. I was glad that they told me that they never had sex. On that I took a deep breath.

"Go ahead and set it up sis," I said.

I felt that I was obligated to do it, and I didn't want anyone else to do it to her. They might take her mind, and she might forget about me.

In the mean time I had to concentrate on my grades. I asked Mr. Robert for his help. He didn't seem like the kind of teacher to tell my business. He seemed like he had a lot of secrets too. I began staying after school twice a week with Mr. Roberts to get my grades up. He turned out to be a pretty cool guy. I never asked him his sexual preference, though. It was obvious from some of his comments that he played on the other team.

No one thought anything about the time I spent with Mr. Roberts because they all knew I loved Gloria.

I was able to pull my grades back up just in time.

We took the SAT test, and we both did very well. I just hope that it was good enough to get us into the right school. A few weeks passed and we all were panicking waiting for the acceptance letters to come.

Gloria called and said she had received hers. She was going to wait until I got mine and we'd open them together.

Two days later, I got mine. Gloria's parents brought her over and we all gathered in the living room. We tossed a coin to see who would open theirs first.

My mother couldn't maintain and yelled "just open it at the same time."

WE did just that. I read mine and she read hers.

I yelled, "I got into Duke."

Gloria yelled, "I'm going to North Carolina State."

We wanted to go to the same school, but we were still happy that we were just a few miles from each other. Our parents were so happy and so proud.

My mother asked Gloria's parents if they wanted to go out for a drink and they grabbed their coats and left us standing there.

"Now is your time", Chenille said.

Take Gloria upstairs and celebrate man. Mom is gone and so are her parents. It's the perfect time.
Gloria heard what my sister said, and I took her hand to go to my bedroom. My sisters clapped as we left the room. They are clowns to the bone.

I closed the door and turned on my stereo. We sat in the bed and began to kiss. I heard someone at my door. I looked, and one of my sisters had pushed a couple of condoms under the door.

"Good looking out," I yelled.

I put my red light in the lamp because I remembered that Morris day said "Red is sexy." We started back kissing and I told her to lay back for me. I didn't know how to do I things so I just opened her legs. I kissed her stomach and kept going lower to her pussy. I had heard that pussy smelled like fish so I was cautious. The closer I got I smelled coconut. It was like a coconut lotion or something. I poked my tongue at her thing, and she jumped a couple of times. This might sound crazy but my sisters had told me what to do earlier.

I began to lick at her real soft and she got really wet down there. She began to close her legs around my head. I quickly grabbed them to keep from suffocating down there. I must have been doing well because she grabbed my head and held it in place. I started licking harder with shorter strokes. I had never heard a woman have an orgasm, but I was about too.

Gloria raised her pussy up to my mouth as to say do it harder. She dropped back down and raised her legs with her hands. That pussy was right there as pretty as I could be. I really went wild on the licking. She grabbed a pillow and covered her face hard. She screamed into it so loud. Her body started jerking and twisting. I just held her there confused about it all. She was breathing kind of hard and long. She then lowered the pillow laughing.

"Damn Marcus, marry me," she said. I thought that I was having an out of body experience.

I got up and put on the condom. I climbed on top of her, and I put it in. She clamped her legs around me like a crab.

"Slow baby," she said. I'm virgin honey.

The only thing that has entered this is a douche for cleaning. It ain't like you little down there either.

I took my time as we kissed and moved. She really got into it and it was over just as fast as it began. I felt like a total idiot. All I could say was "sorry about that."

"I'm not stupid Marcus, and I'm not mad sweetie", she replied. It's your first time too.

The girls at school already told me that guys don't last long on that first orgasm. That's probably why your sister gave you two.

A few minutes later I felt a new hard coming. Gloria took off the old condom and helped me put on another one. We went at it again for about twenty minutes.

I could not hold it when she climbed on top. Just seeing her on top of me excited me too much and it felt so good.

We laid there for about an hour taking and kissing. It ended when my sister knocked at the door.

"OK guys you'll need to clean up and get the sex smell out of your room before our parents get home," she said.

How the hell does she know all of this stuff if she's a virgin? I made a mental note to have a talk with my sister soon about all of this sex knowledge she shares. Our parents returned about couple of hours after the love making.

We were in the living room watching a movie when they walked in. My sister popped popcorn so that the whole house smelled like popcorn instead of sex. I was amazed that she was right. I really have to talk to her ass man.

CHAPTER FOUR

Gloria and I spent a great summer together. We had sex about every weekend until it was time to go off to college. We promised to call every day without tripping and being suspicious of each other. I trusted her and she trusted me. Like I said, I was just a few miles away from her. If she needed me, I was there quickly.

We settled into our studies during the week, and we would hang out on the weekends to get it in. Sometimes I'd go to her place and the next weekend she'd come to mine.

Gloria chose to join the cheer leading team at State. That meant that sometimes she'd be away some weekends and I was cool with that. Their team had made the final four competitions and it was being held in Charlotte, NC. I told Gloria that I couldn't make it because it was my mom's birthday. I wished her all the luck in the world, and I headed to Atlanta to hang with my mother.

When I got there, she was surprised to see me.

"I thought that you would be with your girlfriend this weekend baby", mom said.

"I wanted to surprise you mother and I brought you a gift," I replied. Where are my foolish sisters?

"They drove up to Charlotte for the tournament baby," she said.

They were going to hang with you and Gloria for the weekend. It was supposed to be a surprise for you.

I was standing there looking at my mother's face. She seemed kind of nervous for some reason. Also, I could hear someone in the bathroom. If my sisters were in Charlotte then who the hell was in our bathroom? Just then he walked out of the bathroom. It was Gloria's father. He froze in his tracks not expecting to see me.

"What the fuck is this mom," I asked.

"Watch your language young man," she replied. What the heck are they teaching you at college?

"What the hell is Mr. Daniel's doing here without his wife?" I asked.

"Marcus there is nothing I can say right now that will

make this easier for you or me," said mom.

Mr. Daniels and I have become good friends lately. I
guess you say we are really good friends. There is no
need for me to go into how he and his wife are having
problems because that will mean nothing right now. You
know I'm still getting over your father who I still love so
much. I was lonely Marcus I guess.

"So you cheat with Mr. Daniels to make it all better?" I
said.

What is Mrs. Daniels doing right now? I'm sure she's not
thinking about cheating because she has marital
problems. I wonder what dad is doing right now. I'm
sure he isn't cheating right now because it was easier for
you to screw Mr. Daniels than him tonight.

 "Dads at home thinking about you and him mom," I
said.

He's about to call you and try and work things out. I
know because I spoke with him as I drove down here. I'll
be sure to tell him to forget that idea while I'm driving to
Charlotte.

"Happy Birthday Mother," I yelled.

I stormed out of the door and jumped into the rental
car. I couldn't help but cry because I really missed my
dad being at home. The black woman hate was rising up
again. I needed to talk to someone to ease my nerves. I
called Gloria, and I didn't get an answer.

I didn't think anything of it because it was game weekend and she was a cheerleader.

About that time my cell phone rang. It was Mr. Roberts calling me.

"Hello Marcus," he said.

I was calling all of my former students to see how college life was treating them.

"I'm good Mr. Roberts I guess," I replied.

I think that he knew I was lying some. He could hear the tone in my voice. He told me that he didn't want to pry, but it seemed like I needed an ear. I began to tell him all that happened with my parents and what I saw tonight.

He was very easy to speak with. I began to feel better from the comments and advise he offered me. He told me to have fun with Gloria and if I ever needed someone to listen again that he could be a friend.

I thanked him and continued my drive up to Charlotte. Once I reached Charlotte, I felt excited about surprising Gloria. I needed some loving badly to get this crap off of my mind.

My sister called my phone as I got close to Gloria's dorm.

"Where you at fool?" Tonia asked. Tonia is my youngest sister.

"I'm headed to Gloria's dorm to surprise her." I replied. I also know where you all are.

"Mom told you?" Chenille asked. I know she did Marcus admit it.

"Yea she did," I said. I drove home to surprise her for her birthday, and I was the one who got the surprise.

"You saw Mr. Daniels ha?" she said.

"You fucking knew about this shit?" I yelled.

Why no one tells me shit man? Are you'll in on this shit together or something? What the hell I'm I suppose to say to Gloria? Oh yea, my mom's fucking your dad baby!

"Marcus, you were away from home," she said.

Why tell you so you could freak out and mess up in school? Don't tell Gloria anything man. Don't say shit about this to her. She can't handle it. You know she's a daddy's girl Marcus. Keep this shit to yourself and wait for it to come out on its own. We called Gloria earlier. She was taking a nap. We didn't tell her that we were here. You go see her first and get some ass. Call us when you'll are ready to hang out.

I pulled up and went upstairs to her room. I wanted to catch her napping. We had keys to each other's rooms. That way we could wait for one another if we dropped in. I got to the door, and I heard soft music playing. I put the key in and I turned the handle to open the door.

I peeked in and I died instantly. There was Gloria down on her knees sucking another man's dick. I pushed the door wide open and the light of the hallway lit up the room. He jumped back, and she just looked up at me. I lived so many emotions in a few seconds.

"Marcus baby," she said lightly. I didn't know you were coming baby.

"I see who is coming," I replied.

I slowly backed out of the room and started down the hallway. I left the room key in the door. I could hear her running up behind me. She then stepped in front of me. She stood there in her robe looking straight guilty.

"Marcus, I'm sorry sweetie," she said. It didn't mean anything honey. I love you, Marcus, not him.

"Yes you are sorry Gloria," I replied.

None of this means anything anymore. Have a great life Gloria. He's waiting for you back there. Oh yea, my mom's fucking your dad as we speak. Like father like daughter they always say.

I went down the stairs with such anger. I could not cry anymore tears. All of the shit back home with my mom and then this bullshit here tonight made me super cold on the inside. The hate was boiling over in my heart.

"They cause so much shit for men," I said.

They use men. They break up homes and relationships even marriages.

My heart was double crushed and I wanted revenge. I wanted to make women pay in any way possible.

CHAPTER FIVE

I explained everything to my sisters. They acted like they felt bad for me. They knew that I was crushed. I never heard from Gloria again. I heard through the grapevine that she got pregnant and dropped out.

I finished college and accepted a job back in Atlanta. Even though I sort of hated my mom, I wanted to be close to her because she was getting up in age. I started attending a church there and decided to join the ministry. I needed something to cool the hate I carried in my heart.

I had several ladies in the church to approach me with date offers, but I passed. I had no interest in dating. I had no interest in black women at all.

I started to find solace in the church. I soon became a young deacon and was placed over the kid's Sunday school class. I really loved that part. I adored these children with all my heart. They made me feel needed and kind of special. They looked up to me somehow.

I always wanted to give my parents grandchildren some day. It seems as that dream will never happen for me now. Not with this hatred in my bones. I didn't even want to kiss a woman because I felt that her lips would end up on someone else's dick. Just the thought made me even angrier at women.

I would still receive calls from Mr. Roberts checking on me. Of course I told him about all of the bullshit I had experienced over the last few years. He always knew how to ease the conversation down to a thinking level. He was pretty cool like a reasonable minded dad.

About a year went by, and I was promoted to Minister. I studied Theology as my minor in college. My pastor was very impressed with my knowledge of the Bible. No one knew about my past. All they knew was that I was smart and single with good hair.

One Sunday, a young lady, came to me with her husband. They were a couple about twenty-five or so in age. They asked me to pray with them in the sanctuary. They said that they had been trying to have a child for a couple of years now and have been unsuccessful. She said that she watched how the kids at church respond to me, and they felt that I had a gift for kids.

They told me that God laid it on their heart to have me pray with them. I felt obligated when they stated God told them to ask me. I grabbed the oil from the cabinet and a bottle of holy water. I was going to try anything that day.

We entered the sanctuary, and I asked them to come kneel at the altar.

I anointed both of them with the oil, and I handed Brian the holy water. I told him to pour some into his hand and rub it on his wife's lower stomach area. As he did so, I began to pray for them. I had never prayed at that level ever before. I was in another state of mind and being. It felt like the whole floor shook beneath us.

Tina fell to the floor and screamed. She said it felt like a stomach cramp started. Brian held her, and I continued to call on God for them. We ended the prayer with the usual Amen, and they rose to their feet.

"Thank you Minister Marcus," said Brian. I know God heard you today.

I told them to stay blessed, and I walked them out of the church. I didn't really understand what just took place in that church. I turned around to see the Pastor standing there smiling at me.

"Fine work, Brother Marcus," he said.

I turned back around and headed home confused. I had forgotten about the prayer thing. It had been about a month or more since that day. We were having church service, and I saw Brian and his wife making their way to the front of the church. I didn't think much of it.

When they got to the front the usher gave them a microphone.

"Praise the Lord Saints," Brian said.

The congregation responded "Praise the Lord."

We stand here today to let you all know that we have been blessed. God has performed a miracle with the help of Minister Marcus.

As you all know we have been trying to have a child for years now. God sent us to Brother Marcus and he anointed us and prayed for us right here in this very spot a few Sundays ago.

He gave me some holy water and told me to rub it on my wife's belly. I tell you that when he prayed, the earth shook saints. I'm so glad to tell you today that my wife is pregnant with twins.

The church erupted at that moment. The musicians started a rant, and people started running around the church and shouting down the aisle ways. You would have thought that Jesus himself entered the building. Folks came up to me and started hugging me and crap.

They then pulled me out of my seat and brought me down front. I hugged the couple and told them that I was so happy for them but that was God's miracle, not my own. All of a sudden, I was a Spiritual superman or something. They acted like I had these great healing powers. I was so glad for church to end that day. When it was all over, Pastor called me into his study.

"You have started something now", Pastor said.

You have awakened your calling under God. God has given you something special that so few ever receive. You have the gift of prayer and healing young man.

I didn't know what to say in return. How and why would God give a man like me healing powers? I harbored so much hate in my heart. How could I be useful to God like this? I took Pastors' words to heart, and I left for the day.

I just lay across my bed and wondered why me. All I did was pray for someone. It was the oil and water that made it happen.

I was asked to pray for other people in the church, and things began to happen. People were getting answers to their prayers. The word began to spread to other churches about this anointed minister at our church. I didn't want to even leave the house because people were asking for me to touch them in the strangest places. I almost left the church. I needed some space and some relaxation. I had to change my cell phone and house phone number twice. It got so bad that Pastor had to make an announcement during church service for people to chill with the prayer request. Some people were asking for ridiculous things.

I would take breaks from the drama sometimes by hanging out with Mr. Roberts. He loved the casinos and the gambling scene. It took my mind of back home. Like I said, he was the sensible dad like dude. He was also quite funny. He saw people and life differently than most people.

I needed the humor he offered to my issues.

"I'm glad that you have gotten over all of that hate Marcus," he said.

I said, "Yea, me too."

I didn't choose to go into it, but I haven't gotten over it at all. I still hated women in a certain way. I hadn't been with a woman since that episode with Gloria. I didn't seem to care. The hate was truly real, and I still wanted some kind of revenge.

I moved up higher in the church and was well respected by all. It seems that everyone was trying to get me married off. I had ladies trying to cook me dinner after service and dinner should not include gin and juice for cocktails. Some would even show up to my home with the trench coat thing going. You know the small teddy or lingerie under the coat trick. I admit some of them had it going on but the hate controlled me.

I would lay awake some nights wondering why God gave me a gift like this. I know that he wanted me to have a wife, and I know he knew that I really wanted to have kids one day. How can I use my gift to make it all happen? You know they say that an idle mind is the devils workshop! He was working on me.

CHAPTER SIX

After all my time and work in the church, I was growing tired. I have needed a new quest in my life. That's when Pastor called me into his study.

He explained that his body had grown tired and weary. He wanted to retire and just enjoy the rest of his life with no responsibilities.

He looked me dead in the eye and said, "I want you to lead the church brother Marcus."

He stated that he's been praying on this for awhile now and God put it on his heart that I should become the new Pastor. This is the day that my whole life changed.

You know that saying "what's done in the dark will come to light?"Cover your eyes from the bright lights.

Remember this from chapter one?

"Do me a big favor if you would," said pastor.

"What's that Pastor?" asked Marcus.

"Start a singles committee and find out where all these children are coming from with no fathers", replied Pastor.

It doesn't look good when people come and visit the church. They see all these pretty women and few little men.

"I'll get right on that Pastor McQueen," Marcus replied.

Well, there was no need for a singles committee. There was no need for anything but confession.

The following Sunday two undercover officers entered the church. They wore suits but I know a cop when I see one. I saw them walk in but did not know why and who they were there to see. The officer whispered something to the usher, and I saw the usher point right at me.

The two gentlemen sat down and waited for service to end. Once most of the people left out of the church the officers came towards me.

"Marcus Moore?" the officer asked.

"Yes I am Marcus Moore," I replied. He showed his badge and asked me to come with him.

People were watching in confusion wondering what in

the world I could have done. I followed the men to the door as everybody stood there gazing.

"What's going on here sir?" Pastor asked. Where are you taking him? What's this all about?

"If you must know Pastor," He replied. Mr. Moore is being arrested for crimes against humanity.

I didn't say anything to anyone. They looked at me like they were losing their savior.

"I'll get you a lawyer brother Marcus," someone said.

We'll get you out by tomorrow believe that.

I knew that it was highly unlikely that I would ever see the outside again. The hate I carried had caught up with me. I spent days and nights plotting. I wanted pay back, and the church provided the perfect atmosphere for me to get it. I knew now that soon I would tell my story to the world.

I sat in that cell for a few days and they finally let me see my mother. She came in with tears in her eyes, and right behind her was my pastor. They sat down and just looked at me silently for a few minutes.

"Are you ok son?" she asked.

"I'm good mother," I replied.

Please don't ask anything else. You will know your answers soon.

The Pastor touched my head, and I could smell the oil on his hands. He never said a word, but I could tell that his heart was broken. He was ready to forgive me for whatever I did wrong.

After they walked out, the district attorney walked in. He read me my rights again and told me what my crimes were and how much time they could get me. He asked if I had a lawyer or did I need one appointed to me?

"With all respect, I don't need a lawyer," I said.

I really don't want to go to trial with this. I don't want to embarrass my family nor my church. If it's possible, can you just bring in someone to question me? You can record my confessions and answers and then let a judge decide my fate. I have nothing to hide or lie about.

"I'll have to speak with the judge on this one young man," he said. It may take twenty-four hours for an answer.

I was cool with that. I was tired of hiding everything anyway. All of the damage was done. I could have done more, but my revenge had been settled. Besides, I couldn't hide it for much longer anyway.

The next day the attorney walked in and sat down.

He said that the judge agreed to my request. I guess everyone was curious as to how I did what I did.

They had no real evidence against me. They just couldn't believe what had happened. He told me that they would schedule my hearing for tomorrow at ten in the morning. It would be held in the courtroom, and some people would be present. He also told me that my mother and pastor were requested to attend.

I didn't care at that point because I was blaming my mother and all women for what happened. If they had just been nice people, then I wouldn't be here.

I sat in my cell with my mind racing all night.

CHAPTER SEVEN

They came and took me from my cell. They never hand cuffed me. I guess there was no need. I wasn't a hardened criminal. I still had on the clothes from the other day.

They walked me into the courtroom and the first person I see is my mother. My pastor was sitting to the right with his wife. Then I see my sisters sitting in the back and holy shit. They had my dad with them. Finally, I smiled a little.

The lady directed me to the witness chair, and I sat down. They had a microphone in front of me and adjusted it to fit my mouth height. It was cold in that court man. I looked up at the judge who seemed to be distracted by the notes he was reading about me.

About the time the officer called the court to order. We all rose and the judge asked all to be seated again.

"Hello Mr. Moore," said the judge.

You know why you are here. You have been briefed by our attorney as to the purpose of today's hearing.

You have also agreed verbally and in written form to answer all questions to the best of your knowledge.

You also agreed to this hearing to be recorded and used as evidence for or against you in this court of law. Is this agreed by you sir?

"Yes, your honor," I replied. I have nothing to hide anymore sir.

"Thank you," the judge said. Prosecutor, you may proceed.

"Thanks your honor," she replied.

Mr. Marcus Moore you have been brought here today accused of crimes to humanity. We will explore today the conditions of those charges and why you have been accused.

"Mr. Marcus are you familiar with the Jefferson family?" she asked me.

"Yes I am," I replied.

"Can you tell the court what they requested and how you helped them?" she asked.

"They wanted a baby," I said.

They had heard about me praying for a young lady at my church and how she gave birth to twins. They wanted me to do the same for them, so I did. I told them to keep me posted on the results. Mrs. Darlene Jefferson called me and told me that she did conceive a child.

She sounded so excited about her news, and she said that her husband would learn the news later that day. She couldn't wait for him to get home. He was going to be so happy.

"Mr. Moore, did you know that Mr. Jefferson was unable to make babies?" she asked.

He had an earlier accident in life that enabled him to produce a child. He never told his wife in fear of her not wanting to marry him.

The court gasped all at once. I know they were thinking that I got her pregnant, but I didn't.

"I never had sex with Mrs. Jefferson, if that's what you're thinking," I said.

"I'm not accusing you, Mr. Moore," replied the prosecutor. I'm just laying out my case. I'll continue now thanks.

"Mr. Moore, do you know Theresa Jarvis?"She asked.

"Yes, I know her," I replied.

"Can you tell the court what she wanted and what you did for her?" she asked.

Miss Theresa came to me one Thursday evening after the prayer meeting. She said that she wanted to have a child, but she did not have a husband or boyfriend. In fact she did not want to be married at all. She didn't want to adopt a child because she was afraid of the child might be disturbed or something.

I prayed over her and she conceived a child. She also called and told me the news. She was so excited to the point that she was crying on the phone. She wanted to pay me money, but I refused it.

"Mr. Moore was you aware that Theresa was and still is a virgin?"She asked.

We had the Doctor to examine her and it was clear to him that she has never had sex with anyone. She had to prove to her parents that she was still pure in their eyes. It made you look like God himself Mr. Marcus. You were able to create like without sexual intercourse. How is that I wonder?

"Your honor, I could go on and on," she said.

I could continue naming women, but that would not answer the question that all of us are here to find the answer to.

"Mr. Marcus i have another question", she said.

Would you please tell the court today how you performed your miracles of life?

I paused for a moment and looked around. Everyone looked like they were suspended in time. I took a deep breath and gathered my thoughts.

"Ok, I'll tell you how I did it," I said.

It started back when I first prayed for Brian and his wife. That was truly God's work that day, but I felt that I found my answer.

I hated women and now had the answer to my revenge. I needed to find a way to impregnate women without having sex with them.

After everyone began to trust me and see me as a miracle worker. It was easy to fool them. I invited them over to my home for a private prayer session. I told them that my miracle methods were secret and all powerful and that if they didn't follow my directions, God would not bless them. I also made them promise not to share my methods because it would create false prophets who would try and copy me and that would only harm them and maybe their families.

They swore to be obedient to me and never share the experience. I would have them to go in my bathroom and get into the tub of holy water. They had to be clean and pure before God.

I would later enter with a female douche. I made them believe that this was the water of life in it. I told them that I prayed over this instrument for many hours and kept them in hidden safe to remain unspoiled from man and evil spirits.

After I bathed them, I would ask them to lay back and open their legs in the tub. They had to trust God and me. I told them to repeat "I believe" as I slid the douche into their vagina. As they repeated the words, I would squeeze the warm water into them. Some of them would even have an orgasm from the nostalgia of the moment. I would anoint their head with oil and pray over them.

They would leave, and I would wait for the phone call to see if it worked. I admit that some sessions failed so I called them to try again.

The court could not believe what I was saying on that stand. My dad actually smiled once. I think dad was a freak in his own way.

"So what was in your miracle water Mr. Marcus?" she asked me.

I grew up with a mom and three sisters in our home. I knew that they used a douche often and they were still virgins except mom. I knew if they got tested the doctor would say they never had sex.

It only made sense to use this method. I would remove a condom of frozen sperm from my freezer and place it in very warm water in a douche. I heard about guys getting their sperm frozen for future use if they wanted kids later. I never thought that it would work but when it did, I was amazed.

"Mr. Moore, we had the DNA test performed on these kids and they are not yours," she said.

How do you explain that mystery sir? Where did you get your samples? The court would really like to know.

This was the defining moment that I knew would end my relationship with my family forever. I looked at my dad, and I began to speak.

A couple of years ago I was at a point where I really

hated all women. I didn't want to be touched or kissed by them, not even my own mother or sisters. I had seen things that rotted my stomach and soul. I caught my girlfriend sucking another man's dick in her dorm room. I still see that in my mind this day. It only added to my hate.

I had a friend in my old teacher from high school Mr. Roberts. We hung out a lot at the casinos and such.

No, we did not have a relationship, but he did introduce me to someone. She was absolutely stunning when I laid eyes on her but I could see something was different about her. At the time I didn't care. She made me feel special in every way like I was all that mattered. She listened to me and gave me comfort. It was the first time that I really smiled in a while. She later revealed to me that she was a Trans. She had breast but still had the man parts.

I'm not blaming the alcohol, but it didn't help being as messed up in the head as I was. I'm not blaming the alcohol, but it didn't help being as messed up in the head as I was. I grew close to her or maybe I should say him. Then I included him in my scheme.

I would collect his sperm from the condoms he wore.

I collected about sixteen condoms and froze them. After that I never chose to see him again. It didn't feel right anymore. Not that it ever felt right at all.

"Ok, so now you know," I said.

That's all I choose to say on that note.

I admit to injecting these women with another man's sperm. I admit to having my short gay experience with a Trans. I admit that those women in the church that are pregnant now probably came from my actions and so are some of the kids sitting in the pews. I finally got my pay back, and it felt good but now when I look at it all, I feel like I accomplished nothing but more hurt and pain.

"I'm sorry for the mess I created," I said honestly.

I can't take it back now. I had so much hate inside for mother and what you did. My sisters, I despised you for a time because I knew how you'll were using guys and hurting them.

I wanted to kill you, Gloria, for breaking my heart and crushing it. I never experienced so much pain in such a short time in my life. I thought God hated me when I hated you all.

"I can't say anymore to you," I said.

I asked the judge if it was over and if I could go back to my cell now. I didn't have any more words.

"Does the prosecutor have any more questions?" he asked.

With tears in her eyes, she responded, "No Your Honor."

The whole court was in tears at that moment. I didn't know why, though. There's no way that they could have felt sorry for me with all the destruction that I caused.

They judge dismissed the court and the sheriff came over to get me. I looked at my folks as to see them one more good time. We started towards the door to the jail area.

Someone yelled, "I never stopped loving you, Marcus."

It was Gloria's voice. I knew that voice like the back of my hand.

Because I wasn't looking at her, I could feel the sincerity in her words. I had turned to look at her before I departed the room.

"If you all can forgive me," I said. I can forgive her.

The End

ABOUT THE AUTHOR

Moses is singer, songwriter, producer and animator. He has written and illustrated several children's books available on Amazon Kindle and Books. Today he chooses to write on a more adventurous and thrilling level.
Reading that's sure to satisfy –
AlanBrookCompany, LLC